MAUREEN JENNINGS

Shipwreck

Grass Roots Press

The Good Reads series is funded in part by the Government of Canada's Office of Literacy and Essential Skills.

Grass Roots Press also gratefully acknowledges the financial support for its publishing programs provided by the following agencies: the Government of Canada through the Canada Book Fund and the Government of Alberta through the Alberta Foundation for the Arts.

Grass Roots Press would also like to thank ABC Life Literacy Canada for their support. Good Reads® is used under licence from ABC Life Literacy Canada.

Library and Archives Canada Cataloguing in Publication

Jennings, Maureen
    Shipwreck / Maureen Jennings.

(A Detective Murdoch mystery)
(Good reads series)
ISBN 978-1-926583-26-6

    1. Readers for new literates. I. Title. II. Series. III. Series: Good reads series (Edmonton, Alta.)

PS8569.E562S56 2010   428.6'2   C2010-902004-9

Printed and bound in Canada.

Distributed to libraries and educational and community organizations by
Grass Roots Press
www.grassrootsbooks.net

Distributed to retail outlets by
HarperCollins Canada Ltd.
www.harpercollins.ca

Shipwreck

For Iden Ford, as ever, and for Yannick Bisson,
who is such a wonderful Murdoch

Chapter One

Bill Murdoch had retired from the police department almost a year earlier, but he wasn't enjoying himself. His wife, Julie, had died just before he was to retire, and he was still grieving for her. They had all sorts of plans to travel abroad. He'd even agreed to take a cruise to Alaska. Now, with her gone, he had no desire to go anywhere.

Julie's death was so sudden. It had happened one week before Christmas. Like many long-married couples, they had their routines. He would get up at six, shower, and have his coffee and bran cereal. When he heard Julie stir, he always made a fresh pot of tea and put in some bread to toast. That particular morning, he didn't hear her. She had complained of being out of sorts the night before, and he thought she might be sleeping in.

He never liked to leave without a kiss, so he went upstairs. When he was partway up, he heard an awful thump. He raced the rest of the way to the bedroom. He found her lying half out of bed, her head touching the floor. He rushed over, but he'd seen death before. He knew that she was already dead. It turned out that a clot of blood had gone to her heart, and it had killed her instantly.

He had spent the next months in a state of shock. The police chief suggested that he retire, as he was so close to retirement anyway. So he did, but he only found himself walking from room to room in the house, feeling lost and alone. He and Julie had lived there for over thirty years. He'd lost his purpose. His friends did their best, but nothing could replace his wife. He stopped answering the phone and refused all invitations. Bill was the kind of man who didn't share his feelings easily.

He and Julie had one daughter, Wendy, who had a child. Amy was six years old, the only grandchild, and she was the apple of Bill's eye. She was the one person he didn't cut out of his life after Julie died. He would have liked to have seen more of Wendy, but she was always busy. She was a single mom. She and Keith, her husband, had parted ways about two years before. Wendy was a producer in a film company, and she worked long hours. She had to juggle the duties of her work and the duties of being a mom.

Chapter Two

After Julie's death, Bill's doctor had talked Bill into joining a grief support group. Nice bunch of people, as it turned out. Ten, all told. Only two of them were widowers, men who had lost their wives. The rest were women, mothers and wives for the most part. The leader of the group was a lively young woman named Karen. She was kind, but she refused to let the group members live within their misery for long.

"Life is precious," she said. "We can't waste it. Those we have loved wouldn't want us to."

Bill challenged her when she said that. "You are too young to understand real loss."

"That's not true," she said. "When I was twelve years old, my entire family was killed. My mother and father and my two sisters. They were coming to see me perform in a school concert. A drunk driver side-swiped them. All of them were killed instantly."

"I'm so sorry, Karen," said Bill. "Forgive me for my comment. I didn't know. You seem so cheerful all the time."

"Oh, I still cry on a regular basis. But as I said, we owe it to those who loved us to keep living as well as we can."

Bill knew she was right about that. Julie's zest for life had kept him going through many a dark period. She was like one of those trees with deep roots. No matter how hard the wind blew, she just bent and swayed with its force. She didn't break. That's why her death was so shocking. He'd never dreamed she would be the one to go first.

Karen told all the group members to buy notebooks. She asked them to start writing down what they remembered about the person they had lost. It was a healing exercise, she said. Bill had doubts at first, but again, she was right. He found he enjoyed writing. All sorts of memories came back to him about the long life he and Julie had

had together. The group members shared their writing every week, and those Friday afternoons were the best he'd had for a long time.

At the end of the grief support course, Karen took Bill aside. "Don't stop writing, Bill," she said. "You should write down all your family memories. They are a wonderful gift to leave to your daughter and grandchild."

"I'm not sure how interested my daughter, Wendy, is."

"I bet she will be interested once you show your stories to her."

"Where would I start?"

"Go back as far as you like. You told us that all the men in your family have been police officers, right back to your great-grandfather. Why do you think he chose to join the police force?"

"Good question. The pay was poor and the hours were long. But something made him stick it out, and he became a detective. I have a photograph of him from 1895. He looks like a good person."

"Wow," said Karen. "Sounds like you've got a lot you could write about."

"Well…I don't know…."

"Come on, Bill. It would be a good exercise for you."

So Bill started to write, and he found that his great-grandfather's story came quite easily to him. He enjoyed trying to get into the heart and mind of his ancestor.

He told Wendy what he'd written. She said she wanted to read it, but as yet, she hadn't found time.

Chapter Three

The evening was cold and wet. Sleet was slamming against the windows. Bill felt miserable. Tomorrow would be the first anniversary of Julie's death, and he dreaded spending Christmas without her. He warmed up a frozen pasta dinner from the supermarket. He thought about writing some more, but he couldn't settle into it. The hockey game was due to come on in a minute. If the Maple Leafs won, watching the game would be even better for his mood than writing.

The phone rang. He answered it.

"Hi, Dad, it's me."

Bill groaned to himself. He loved Wendy, but he knew from experience that when she called on a Saturday evening, she wanted something. He was right.

"Dad, I hate to ask you this on such short notice, but my babysitter has let me down. She broke her ankle at the skating rink. She's in the hospital."

"Well, that's a good excuse," said Bill. "Let me guess. You want me to babysit?"

"Oh, Dad, will you? I'd cancel going out, but it's a special office party, and I really shouldn't miss it."

Normally, Bill was only too happy to be with his granddaughter, but tonight the hockey game was a special one. He didn't really want to go out in this miserable weather, either.

"I don't suppose Keith could do it, for once? He is Amy's father, after all."

There was a little silence on the other end of the line.

"In fact, it's Keith's office party I'm going to," Wendy said.

Another silence. "You didn't tell me you were getting back together."

"I'm not really sure we are, that's why. We're trying to start all over again. Just go on some dates. That sort of thing. Besides, I didn't tell you because I know how you feel about him."

"Hey, Wendy. It's your life. I'm not the one he cheated on. I'm not the one who was dumped without notice. That was you, my girl. But maybe you can forgive him for that. And for being an empty-headed, self-centred idiot who's only interested in getting rich fast. If you can forgive all that, you deserve angel's wings."

"Dad. Please. Keith has changed. He's been thinking about things. He says he misses Amy and me."

"Really? You could have fooled me. I thought he forgot her last birthday."

Wendy sighed. "He's changed, Dad. He really has. And he is the father of your granddaughter. Surely that counts for something?"

"Amy is the only reason I haven't slugged the guy."

In the background, Bill heard the sound of a doorbell ringing.

"That's Keith now," Wendy said. "Dad, will you do this for me? You know how much Amy loves you."

"I was planning to come over tomorrow."

"I can't get anybody else on such short notice," Wendy said. "You can stay overnight and spend the day with her tomorrow. She's still not feeling quite herself since she got the chicken pox. She will be thrilled to see you."

"I was planning to work on the story I told you about."

"Bring it with you. You could read it to her. She'd like that."

"It's not a kid's story," Bill said.

"You can skip over the parts she might not understand." Wendy sighed. "Please, Dad. I'm really stuck. When Amy falls asleep, you can work here. You can use my computer if you like."

"No, I'm still at the pen and ink stage."

"Seriously, Dad, I'm really stuck."

"Okay, okay. You've got to give me a half-hour to get my things together. Maybe Keith could wait in the car."

"Dad. For goodness' sake! I'll see you in half an hour, then."

She hung up with a slam.

Bill felt bad. He didn't want her to feel torn between her father and her ex-husband. However, he really couldn't stand his former son-in-law. He hoped Wendy would see the light soon.

Chapter Four

When Bill got to Wendy's house, she already had her coat on. Keith was nowhere to be seen. Wendy gave her dad a peck on the cheek.

"Thanks, Dad. Amy is all ready for bed. She's in her PJs. We won't be late."

"Wendy, I'm sorry for sounding hard-hearted. I just want the best for you."

"I know you do, Dad."

Wendy smiled. But she seemed sad. Then she picked up her purse and gloves, blew him a kiss, and left.

Bill went upstairs to Amy's room. She was in bed, looking at one of her picture books. She looked thinner since having chicken pox. There were still scabs on her face and arms.

"Granddad! Mommy said you were coming. Oh, goodie!"

He walked over to the bed and gave her a kiss. She seemed a little hot to him. Her cat, a black and white ball of fluff, glanced at him and meowed. Bill ruffled its hair.

"Hiya, Boots. Catch any mice today?"

The cat started to clean its paws and refused to answer.

"How are you feeling, sweetheart?" Bill asked Amy.

"I'm still itchy, but Mommy says I can go back to school next week." She looked up at him. "What do you want to do tonight, Granddad?"

"What do you want to do, Amy?"

"Hmm. My eyes are tired, so no TV. I think I'd like a story."

"Sure thing. What would you like to hear?"

"Mommy said you are writing down your memories. I'd like to hear them."

"They're not exactly memories, Amy, just stories I'm writing about the family. I wasn't even born when my story took place."

She looked puzzled. At six years old, Amy was still trying to make sense of life. She found it hard to understand how somebody who was here, now, hadn't always been alive.

"What's the story called?"

"Shipwreck."

"And what's it about?"

"It's about the early life of my great-grandfather, William Murdoch."

"That's the same name as you, except you're called Bill instead of William."

"That's right. The name William is passed down through the family."

"Why wasn't I named William?"

"It's a boy's name."

"No, it's not. There's a girl in my class named Billie."

"You're named after the first William's wife. Her name was Amy."

His granddaughter wrinkled up her forehead. "We're learning this sort of thing in class. Making a family tree. You are my grandfather." She started to count on her fingers. "That means your great-grandfather would be my great-great-great-grandfather. And his wife, Amy, would be my great-great-great-grandmother. Three greats." She beamed.

"Well done, Amy, well done. You're right. The first William Murdoch was born in 1861. About 150 years ago."

"He must have been very old when he died."

Bill decided to let that pass. He could understand her point of view.

She thought for a moment. "Was he a policeman?"

"Yes, he was. He was a detective."

"Like you were?" Amy asked.

"Yep."

"Cool. None of the other kids at school have grandfathers who were detectives. Did you catch bad men who killed people?"

"Yes, I did," replied Bill.

"Lots?"

"Should have been more, but yes, I caught lots."

"Did you see dead people, with their blood and guts hanging out?" Amy asked.

Bill made a mental note to talk to Wendy about the kind of television programs Amy was watching.

"No, no guts."

She looked disappointed. "Any dead people?"

"Yes, some."

She scratched at a chicken pox scab. "Did you have chicken pox when you were a kid, Granddad?"

"I sure did."

"Did I get it from you, then?"

"No, of course not. You don't catch chicken pox from somebody who used to have it. You catch it from somebody who has it now."

"Like Sammy Dutton, in my class. He came to school with spots all over him. They were even in his hair. Miss Dillon had a fit and sent him right home. She asked him why he'd come to school when he was so sick. You know what he said, Granddad?"

"What?"

"He said his mom hadn't noticed his spots, and it was much nicer to be at school. Do you call them pox?"

"Yes, you can do that. Or spots. Sorry about Sammy."

"He smells bad sometimes. Sophie sits behind him. She told the teacher. Miss Dillon said that was because he didn't have a mommy or daddy who could take care of him the way our mommies and daddies do." Amy looked into her grandfather's eyes. "Why can't she, Granddad? Why can't Sammy's mommy look after him?"

Bill stroked her hair. "I don't know the answer to that, sweetheart. Sometimes life wears people down."

She wriggled away from him. "Sophie says that Sammy's mommy doesn't have a husband. Not even one who lives somewhere else, like my daddy. She says Sammy's mommy is very young."

"Is that so?"

"Mm-hmm."

"Okay, little monkey. It's getting late. Are you sure you want to hear a story now?"

Amy, who had been leaning against her grandfather's arm, sat up straight.

"I'm very sure. Why did the first William Murdoch become a detective?"

"That is what I'm going to tell you, if I ever get a chance. I think you could say that he became a detective because of a shipwreck."

A sudden gust of wind threw pellets of snow against the window. Outside, the wind shook the trees. The branches scratched at the glass, as if they wanted to come in.

Amy snuggled further down under her covers.

"Daddy stayed over last night. It was too cold for him to go to his own house."

Bill raised his eyebrows. "I see."

"It's nice when Daddy stays over," said Amy. "Mommy smiles more. She says he is coming back to live here."

"Oh, is he?" So much for Wendy and Keith going out on test dates. She hadn't mentioned this earlier.

"That means I won't have to sleep at his house anymore," continued Amy. "I don't like that because I have to leave Boots here. Daddy sneezes when Boots is around. He said that's why he had to go and live in his own house." Amy frowned. "Is that true, Granddad? I hope he won't make Boots live somewhere else."

Bill scratched the cat's head. "Let's not worry about that now. Are you ready for the story?"

Amy nodded. "Yes. Are you ready, Boots?"

The cat purred. Bill took that as a yes.

He tucked Amy's comforter around her shoulders. "Warm enough?"

"Yes, Granddad. Please start."

"Now, listen up, and don't interrupt unless there's something you don't understand."

"Okay, Granddad. Daddy interrupts all the time, and it sure is irritating."

The word was too adult for a six-year-old. Amy had to be repeating something her mother said. Bill made another note to speak to Wendy. She had to think before she talked about her own problems in front of a bright child like Amy.

Chapter Five

Bill began his story. "The weather was very much like this, gloomy, cold, and snowy, but much, much worse. The snow was deep on the ground. Even though it was the Day of the Nativity — that is another word for Christmas..."

"I know that. It means native," said Amy.

"Er, no. It means the day of birth. The day Jesus was born."

"And Santa Claus. The day Santa was born."

Bill groaned to himself. Amy was a child of her time. He decided to leave that subject alone for now, too.

"Here we go," continued Bill. "The village was just outside of Halifax. That's on the east side of Canada..."

"I know that, Granddad. It's in Newfoundland."

"No, it's in Nova Scotia."

"Well, I was close."

One thing that bothered Bill about the kids of today was that they couldn't admit they were wrong. Too many well-meaning teachers giving them a mark for trying, instead of saying, "Wrong. That is the wrong answer."

"You're frowning, Granddad," said Amy. "Can we go on with the story?"

"As I was saying, the village where this story takes place was in Nova Scotia. It was Christmas Day. Christmas morning, to be exact. Very early. The sun wasn't even up yet. All night long, the fierce wind, heavy with snow, had swept in from the sea. Only half of the people who belonged to my great-grandfather's church came to Mass. The second altar boy was ill. Do you know what an altar boy is, Amy?"

"No."

"An altar boy helps the priest."

"Like I help Mommy in the kitchen when she's making dinner?"

Bill smiled. "Something like that. So on this day, when there were usually two boys who helped, there was only one. His name was William Murdoch."

"My great-great-great-grandfather. Three greats," interrupted Amy.

"Hush. Listen up. William Murdoch was twelve years old when our story takes place. He lived with his mother and his father, who was a fisherman. He had a younger sister and a younger brother."

"I asked Mommy if I can have a sister," said Amy. "She said she'll think about it."

Bill placed his finger on his lips. "Shh! As I was saying, William had a sister and a brother. Bertie, his brother, was handicapped. He was what people back then called slow. His mind worked in a simple way. That day, William's family was in the church, except for his father, whose name was Harry. Harry never went to church. Not anymore.

"So far, Will had done his duties as an altar boy well. He hadn't forgotten anything or made any mistakes. But the church was so cold, he could see his own breath on the air. His stomach was rumbling, because he had not eaten yet."

Amy put up her hand as if she were in school. "Why not? Were they poor, like Sammy's mommy? He sometimes comes to school without breakfast. I always have my oats in the morning. Did they have oats in the olden time?"

"Yes, they did. William wasn't poor. He could have oats in the morning. But he hadn't eaten yet because people believed that not eating before Mass was a sign of love for God. The church called this fasting, going without food for a short time."

Amy was looking puzzled. Bill decided to leave religious explanations to her mother. "Okay, he said, "Back to the story…"

Will was hungry, and he let his mind wander briefly to the Christmas dinner his mother had made. They were to eat it later in the day. But he tried to focus on his church duties. He knew his mother was watching him. For her sake, he tried to make his face look serious. As if he was thinking good thoughts.

He wasn't sure he truly felt good. He had come close to fighting with his own father. The night before, Harry had made the evening miserable for his family. He made fun of each of them, but especially Will's brother, Bertie. Poor, simple Bertie. Harry's tone and words stung like whip lashes. His hands were ready to hit or slap at any moment. Harry was always angry when he was drunk.

Suddenly, William saw that Father Keegan was moving toward him. He knew he had fallen behind in his duties. Quickly, he went to the table for the glass bottles containing the water and wine. He handed them to the priest, remembering, just in time, to kiss each one while thinking about God. Will was wearing a cassock, a long black robe that reached to his feet. As he turned to go back for the linen cloth and basin, his foot got caught in his robe, and he tripped. Will felt the hem of his robe tear away. His face went red. How could he be so clumsy? His mother would be ashamed of him.

When Will finished his task and made it back to Father Keegan, the priest held out his hands. William poured some water over them, catching the drops in the basin. The priest's nails were cracked and dirty, and his thumbnail was bruised. In this small village, Father Keegan was expected to do his own wood chopping and simple carpentry. He wasn't very good at that kind of work. Behind his back, some of the men even made fun of him for his lack of skill.

When the old village priest had died, Father Keegan had been sent from a parish in Halifax. He was a tall, thin man of about fifty years of age. He was also lame from a badly mended leg. Walking was hard for him. Gossip had it that Father Keegan had received his call to the priesthood later in life. Before that, he had been a doctor in the Union army during the American Civil War.

Some people said he had been shot in the leg by a Rebel soldier. Gossip also claimed that he had been married before he became a priest, but his wife and children had died. Nobody knew for sure whether that was true, either. The priest was not the kind of man who would chat about his own life. People in the parish sometimes asked him over for a meal and put a glass of hot cider in his hand. He still didn't open up.

The biggest complaint about Father Keegan was that he was too strict in his views about how people should behave. There was always a lot of muttering when people met up with each other after confession. The men, especially, thought that certain sins were only human nature. They weren't worth talking about, really. In this group of sins the men placed the times when they were mean to a neighbour. Or cheated the storekeeper. Or didn't help the poor of the parish. The angry words they sometimes spoke to their wives or children. The lustful thoughts about other men's wives. These were just human weaknesses. Nobody's perfect.

Father Keegan didn't seem to care as much about things that had bothered the former priest, like how many times they missed Mass or ate meat on Friday. But he cared a lot about how the people of his parish treated each other.

Will admired Father Keegan, but the priest made Will nervous. He had high standards.

Chapter Six.

"I thought this story was about a shipwreck," said Amy.

"It is," answered Bill. "You must be patient. The shipwreck is coming."

Father Keegan finished drying his hands on the linen cloth and turned back to the altar. The most important part of the Mass was coming. It was called the Canon, the point from which there was no turning back. Will went to his position and knelt on the edge of the platform.

Suddenly, the church door opened with a bang. A man Will knew from the village burst in. The wind gusted behind him, carrying him along. The man started yelling as soon as he got inside.

"Ship's sinking, down on the rocks. We need to put out the lifeboat."

Father Keegan had been about to raise the thin wafer of bread that is called the Host. He turned in shock at this intrusion. Only a man not of the Catholic faith would have dared to intrude at that moment.

The man shouted, "She's a three-master, a sailing ship that's been blown onto the rocks. Looks like the crew got into the rowboat, but they're not doing too well in this wind." He looked around the church. "Who'll come to man the lifeboat with me?"

There was a rustle through the crowd sitting in the long wooden pews, but nobody moved. All looked toward the priest.

Father Keegan spoke. "I cannot stop the Mass." He glanced quickly around at his flock. "I will give communion as fast as I can. But Our Lord would not wish innocent souls to be lost for want of a boat. All you men are excused. Bob Markham, will you ring the warning bell? Women, children, and the elderly will stay here in the church until the service is finished."

He turned his back on the man who had burst in, knelt, and began to pray.

Behind him, the men shuffled out of their pews, bent at the knee, and bowed their heads toward the altar. Then each one hurried out down the aisle to the church door. Will, too, was filled with excitement. This was by no means the first ship to crash against the rocky coast. The villagers always did everything they could to rescue those in danger. Earlier in the summer, three parishes in the area had come together, even though they were of different faiths. Together they had built a lifeboat.

Will wanted to be down on the shore himself. It was all he could do to remain calm. Above him, the church bell rang out, warning the rest of the village that there was a ship in trouble.

Chapter Seven

Father Keegan went through the rest of the Mass as fast as he could. He spoke so quickly that his Latin words became impossible to follow in the prayer book. All the bending and kneeling was hard on the priest's crippled leg, and he had to stifle his groans. People came to the altar rail to receive communion, but only the most pious of the women had their minds on what they were doing. The wind rattled at the windows, reminding them of what was happening on the shore. Finally, the priest ended the service with his blessing.

A quiet chatter broke out, but Father Keegan held up his hands for quiet. "Now then. All of you women bring as many blankets and dry clothes as you can spare. I will make our parish hall available, and anyone who is injured may be brought here."

He beckoned to Will. "Come and help me remove my robes."

Will followed Father Keegan to the dressing room behind the altar. His mother, his sister, and his brother left the church. Will suspected that the longed-for Christmas feast was going to be divided among those in greater need. He had to push away a tiny flash of anger. He had been looking forward to that roast goose.

Will and the priest changed out of their church robes as quickly as they could. Will had come to the church in his best suit, which was made of good thick wool. However, he knew his mother would excuse him if he got it dirty. Tearing the hem of his church robe would make her scold him, but getting dirty saving shipwrecked sailors wouldn't.

Father Keegan and Will left the church, the wind grabbing them and biting into their faces. Bent double, they struggled to the cliff's edge. There, a path led down to the shore. In the dim light, Will could just make out the shape of a small sailing ship. One of the masts had snapped off.

The wind had driven the ship forward and jammed the bow on the ragged teeth of the rocks. Now the deck sloped toward the ship's rear end, which the hungry waves battered. The crew had managed to get into a little rowboat. A sailor held up a lantern as high as he could, and the light bobbed up and down. One moment Will and Father Keegan could see it, the next moment the waves hid it from them.

"How many do you see, Will?" asked Father Keegan. "I count six souls."

"Yes, Father. They don't seem to be making headway at all."

The villagers had launched the lifeboat, and it, too, was being tossed about, the oars sawing at air over and over again. The five men aboard struggled to keep the boat under control.

"Come on," said Father Keegan.

The priest started down the steep path to the shore. William followed close behind him. They both slipped and slid on the wet stones. They'd hardly got halfway down when they saw a huge wave smash sideways into the little rowboat. It flipped up and over like a toy. All of the people it carried were tossed out into the sea.

Chapter Eight

Father Keegan paused and made the sign of the cross in the direction of the overturned rowboat. "May the Lord have mercy," he said.

The lifeboat was also being blown around, and away from the damaged ship. One of the men in it lifted his lantern. The light shone on a shape in the icy grey water. Someone was clinging to a piece of driftwood. Two of the men leaned over and pulled the person aboard. William saw, with surprise, that it was a woman. Almost at once, the lifeboat began to head back to shore, helped by the wind.

A crowd had gathered on the shore, and several men rushed forward to help pull in the boat. One of them threw out a line. The man in the front of the lifeboat grabbed it. Quickly, he tied it to the boat.

The priest, who wasn't strong enough to help pull, took command. "Heave," he cried. "All together! Heave!"

Every time he shouted "Heave," the men pulled with all their strength, leaning back until their behinds almost touched the sand.

Will had gripped the rope along with the other men. He felt as if he were fighting the sea god himself in a deadly struggle. The lifeboat, out there on the waves, seemed tiny and as slight as a wooden toy. The rowers dug in with their oars whenever they could. More villagers, including a couple of the younger women, threw their weight into the pull.

Father Keegan kept up his chant. "Heave! And heave!"

Finally, they had the bow of the boat on the beach. The men on board placed the woman they had rescued into the strong arms of a big fisherman. Will had a glimpse of a white face, thin and young. The fisherman carried her to the big sheet of canvas that had been laid on the sand at the ready. He put the girl down gently, and the village women surrounded her at once.

"We must go back out, Father," said one of the rescuers. He was a rough-looking fellow with a thick beard. He had been one of the first members of the church to answer the call for help. "There are others out there. The lassie is so bad that we had to bring her in first."

The five men, each wearing a cork life-belt, climbed back into the lifeboat. Those on the shore pushed them out to sea again. If anything, the wind was fiercer than before. Will wasn't sure they would be able to get out to the rocks where the ship was wedged.

Father Keegan went to where the young woman lay and bent over her. Will saw the priest's body stiffen with alarm. He ran over to him, and Father Keegan drew him close. The priest had to shout into Will's ear in order to be heard above the roar of the wind and the sea.

"We have to move her at once. She is with child, and, by the look of her, she's near her time. We'll get her to the hall. I want you to go and get Mrs. Cameron, the midwife."

At this point, Amy twisted around in the bed. Bill paused to see if she was still listening. She was.

"I hope she doesn't die, Granddad."

"You'll have to wait and see. Do you want me to stop now, and go on with the story tomorrow?"

"No. I must know what happens. Did they save all the others?"

Bill was beginning to feel sorry he had started this story. Amy was a child. It might not be fair to tell her a story that didn't have a happy ending, like the princess stories she enjoyed so much.

"Sweetheart, it's getting late. Perhaps you should go to sleep now."

Amy sat up in her bed. "Granddad. I am not tired. I cannot go to sleep unless I know what happened to all the poor people in the shipwreck. Could they swim?"

"Er…I don't know."

"I can swim now. I would have been able to get to shore."

He pinched her cheek gently. "I'm sure you would have." He folded up his papers. "Look at you. You can hardly keep your eyes open. We will finish this in the morning."

"Perhaps Mommy would like to hear it as well?"

"We'll ask her."

He tucked in the covers. Amy's eyes were already closing. He kissed her forehead.

"Nighty-night, sweetie."

He switched off the light and left quietly. Downstairs, in the den, he turned on the television set. He could catch some of the game at least.

Chapter Nine

Amy was up early, and Bill went into the kitchen to help with breakfast. Wendy was already there, wearing her dressing gown. For a moment, she looked so much like Julie, her mother, that Bill's heart jumped.

"Did you have a good time last night?" he asked.

"It was all right." She sniffled. "I think I'm coming down with a cold."

"Granddad was telling me a wonderful story," said Amy. "It's sad, though. The people on the boat couldn't swim, and they drowned."

Wendy looked over at her father.

"Good thing I can swim," continued Amy. "And William, the first William, my three-times-great-granddad, has gone to get the midwife."

"Do you know what a midwife is, Amy?" her mother asked.

She nodded. "A woman who is almost a wife."

Wendy smiled. "Not exactly. A midwife is a woman who helps babies to be born."

"I think I'll be a midwife when I grow up," said Amy.

Wendy glanced up at the kitchen clock. "You know what, Amy? Your favourite cartoon is coming on in a minute. Would you like to go into the den and watch it?"

"What about Granddad's story?"

"I'll listen to it for you. And I can tell you later what happened."

"Okay."

Amy picked up the cat and carried it into the den.

Bill smiled at Wendy. "Whew. Thanks. I told you it was a story for adults. I was getting into deep water in more ways than one." He handed her the pile of papers. "Here. You can read it when you like."

"No, Dad. Read it to me. I loved it when you read to me when I was a child."

Bill was pleased. "Okay. Why don't you go upstairs and get back in bed. You do look as if you're coming down with a cold. I'll bring you a hot lemon drink, and I'll read you the rest of the story."

"That sounds lovely. You've always made the best hot lemon drinks."

Wendy called to her daughter, "Amy, Mommy's going back to bed for a bit. Will you be all right?"

"Of course, Mommy."

Wendy went upstairs while Bill made her the hot drink. He took it up to the bedroom, and he sat on the chair next to the bed while Wendy sipped it.

"Delicious." She snuggled down under the covers in the same way that Amy had done the night before.

"I'm ready."

Bill quickly filled Wendy in on the story so far. Then he went on.

William took a long time to bring Mrs. Cameron, the midwife, to the parish hall. The snow was deep, and she lived on the edge of the village. She was an old woman and not too steady on her feet. At first, she was nervous about going into a building that belonged to Catholics. She herself was a Baptist. But Will told her that the hall was only a building, like any other. It was the church that was holy. So with Mrs. Cameron clinging to Will's arm, the two of them set off through the snow.

Finally they arrived at the hall. When they got inside, Will saw that the village women had been busy. They had hung a curtain at the rear of the hall to make a private space for the young woman from the sea. That was how William had started to think about her.

Will saw several more sheets of canvas laid out on the floor. These tarpaulins would receive the dead. But there were also some welcoming touches. Pine branches hanging on the doors scented the air. A big log fire already blazed in the hearth. Will's mother was with the other village women, putting food out on a wooden table. If there were survivors, they would need food. And so would the rescuers.

Will had been right about the Christmas roast goose dinner. He could see the pot his mother had cooked it in. His stomach grumbled, reminding him that he hadn't eaten since last night. But he had no time to eat now.

His mother called him over. "Take these buckets of water to the fire, Will. We need to boil water."

Other tasks followed, so he couldn't return to the shore right away, although he wanted to. Every so often, he heard a cry of pain coming from behind the curtain where the young woman was lying.

After what seemed a long time, Father Keegan entered the hall, leading a grim line of men. They were bringing in the bodies from the doomed boat. They laid them on the tarpaulins and covered each man with a blanket. There were five corpses.

Gathered along the wall were the people who belonged to the church, the parishioners. They stood side by side with the rest of the villagers who had answered the church bell's call for help. All of them watched silently.

Father Keegan began to make the sign of the cross over each corpse. The Methodist minister and the pastor from the Baptist church were both doing their own praying. However, this was Father Keegan's hall, and out of respect, they stayed back.

The priest beckoned to Will. "You are a clever boy, William Murdoch, and your handwriting is clear. The people who have died will all have loved ones somewhere. Their mothers and wives will want to claim them. We cannot allow any confusion."

Father Keegan's eyes were dark with fatigue. He nodded in the direction of the watching villagers. "These are good people. They did not hesitate to risk their own lives. But they are also only human. And poor. Taking from the dead is a great temptation." He sighed. "We must make sure our people do not give in to that temptation. You and I will examine each of these bodies, and we will make careful notes. First, we will describe what each man looks like. Then we will list whatever we find in his pockets or on his person." He smiled slightly. "You are not afraid of the dead, are you, my son?"

"No, Father."

Even if he had been afraid, Will would have died himself before admitting it. He wanted the priest to be proud of him, and his mother, too. She was watching with the other villagers.

"Go into the office, and on my desk you will see a notebook and pencil. Bring them here."

Chapter Ten

Will returned with the notebook and pencil. Father Keegan had put up a rope barrier around the area where the dead lay.

The priest removed the blanket covering one of the bodies. "Write this down: Man of about forty-five years of age, five feet seven or eight inches tall, wide shoulders. Grey streaked hair and full beard. Large nose, slightly crooked." He lifted one of the man's eyelids. "Brown eyes." He gently opened the mouth. "Two front teeth missing, tobacco stains. He has lost the tip of his right forefinger, but it's an old injury. Got all that, Will?"

"Yes, Father."

"Good lad. The clothes on this man are as follows: Canvas jacket, navy jersey, waterproof trousers, and rubber boots."

Will wrote it all down as fast as he could. Father Keegan began to empty the man's pockets and spread out the contents on the floor. "Clay pipe and tobacco pouch of good leather, linen handkerchief, a spyglass. A good one, made of brass." He fished inside the inner pockets of the jacket and pulled out some pieces of paper. They were surprisingly dry.

"As I thought, this good man was the captain of the ship. He has kept his papers close to his heart. They are important documents, the record of the ship's load. The cargo was fresh fish and dried cod." He looked at the papers again. "Ah. I wondered why there was a woman on board such a vessel. It says here that there were two passengers, a merchant, and his wife. Our young lady must be the wife. The captain does not name them, but he does say how much the man paid for their fare. Cheap, really, but then this was a rough ship."

Will and Father Keegan took care of the remaining four bodies, one by one, in the same careful way. All were sailors, members of the crew. One looked not much older than William.

"His mother will weep," said Father Keegan.

The parish hall door banged open, and more of the weary rescuers came in. They were carrying two more bodies, each wrapped in a tarp.

"We managed to reach the ship, Father," said one of them, a short, weather-beaten man and fellow Catholic. "It was stuck tight on the rocks, but it will be gone soon. The seas are breaking it to pieces."

"Good work, Saul. Put them at that end," said Father Keegan.

The men lowered their burdens carefully. Saul pointed down to one body. "This man hadn't even made it to the rowboat. He was trapped below deck. We found him lying in one of the cabins."

The second tarpaulin appeared to be particularly heavy, and the men placed it on the ground with sighs of relief. Father Keegan opened that tarp first. He revealed the body of a young man, his blond hair and moustache full of bits of seaweed. He was wearing a thick wool coat trimmed with lush fur at the collar and cuffs, all soaked.

"That one there in the fancy coat had climbed onto the reef," said Saul. "He must have slipped, because he drowned stuck between two rocks. He'd been smarter to throw off his coat, if you ask me." He took out a handkerchief and wiped his round face, which was sweating in spite of the cold. "I do believe that's the lot. All dead except for the woman we brought in earlier. God rest their souls."

Saul blessed himself, touching the fingers of his right hand to his forehead, his breastbone, and the left and right sides of his chest in the shape of a cross.

The rescuers stepped back. Father Keegan and Will went to examine the last body, the man found on board the ship.

At that moment, the thin cry of a newborn came from behind the curtain. Everybody in the hall stopped what they were doing at the sound. Several of them, the Catholics, blessed themselves. The Methodist minister clasped his hands together and looked toward heaven in prayer.

Mrs. Cameron came out from behind the curtain. "Father Keegan?" she said quietly. "We have need of you, Father. At once. The girl has delivered her baby, but I do believe she is not long for the living. Her colour's very bad."

"And the infant?"

"'Tis small, but she appears healthy enough."

"A girl child, then?"

"Yes, Father."

The priest spoke to Will. "Come. If you are not afraid of the dead, you can tolerate the dying, even if it is a woman."

Mrs. Cameron drew aside the curtain, showing them the mattress on the floor where the young woman rested, covered by a blanket. Her clothes had been removed, and her naked arms lay outside the covers. The village women had unpinned her hair, which was a deep brown. Although it was still damp from the sea, Will could see that it would normally have been thick and glossy. Her eyes were closed, and she seemed to be hardly breathing. There was a purple bruise on the side of her jaw.

"I think her ribs are broken. Her labour was very painful," said Mrs. Cameron. "But she hardly complained. Poor little thing, she is still a child herself, if truth be told."

"Did she tell you her name?" the priest asked.

"All she could say was her Christian name. It is Abigail." The midwife lifted the girl's limp hand. She was wearing a wedding band richer than any Will had seen before. Rubies on a wide circle of gold. "Whoever she is, she married well. The nightclothes we took off her are fine indeed."

The girl breathed in short gasps, and her skin was chalk white. Will's heart went out to her. Even he knew she was dying.

She opened her eyes, as blue as any he had seen. She saw the priest, and her face twisted with fear.

"Father, why are you here? Am I to die, then?" Her voice was a whisper.

"You are of the Catholic faith, child?"

"Yes, I am."

The priest spoke gently. "Then I must prepare you to meet your maker, my daughter."

Father Keegan reached out and made the sign of the cross on her forehead with his thumb.

"Do not be afraid, my child. This day, you will rest in Paradise with Our Lord Jesus Christ."

A sob escaped her throat.

"Were any saved?" she asked.

"Alas, no," Father Keegan answered. "The men just now brought in the last two. One, I believe, is your husband."

Her eyes widened. "My husband?"

"He is blond, is he not, with a full moustache? He was wearing a fur-trimmed coat."

"He is dead?"

"Yes, my child."

Tears sprang to her eyes. She turned her head and was so still that Will wondered if she had already slipped away.

Abigail opened her eyes again. Her voice was so weak they could hardly hear her.

"All died, you say?"

"Alas, yes, my child. Seven souls, all told."

She stirred slightly. "Did they all die instantly? Did you speak to any, Father?"

"I did not. There was no chance."

A long sigh came from her lips. Then she said, "Will my baby live?"

"Mrs. Cameron says she is healthy. Do you want to hold her?"

She nodded. The midwife picked up the tiny creature, tightly wrapped in a blanket. Only the little red wrinkled face was visible. She placed the baby in the crook of the young mother's arm, and Abigail touched her baby's cheek tenderly.

"She has not had the best entry into this sad world, has she?" Again, the young woman looked up at the priest. "The man in the coat, the blond man…"

"Your husband?"

"He was a good man. He saved me. He gave up his place in the boat for me. His name is John."

Father Keegan shifted to a more comfortable position so he could straighten his stiff leg.

The young mother kissed her infant on the forehead, soft as snow touching the ground.

The priest called over the midwife. "Mrs. Cameron, one of the village women, Mrs. Pierce, lost her own child but a week ago. She grieves the loss. I want you to have her brought here. Her breasts will still have milk."

Will blushed at the words and the image, and he lowered his head.

Abigail spoke again. "There is money," she continued. "It is sewn into the seams of the fur-trimmed coat. I must ask you to claim it on behalf of my infant child. I heard what you said to the midwife. Please, Father, promise me the money will go to that woman who will be her wet nurse. I want her to take care of my child."

"Surely you yourself have a family who will take the baby in?"

"No, I have no one."

"Your husband, then?"

"No, he has no family, either."

"What is your name, and where do you live?" Father Keegan asked.

She didn't reply but licked her lips. "I am so thirsty."

Father Keegan reached over to a table where somebody had placed a glass of wine. He brought it to her lips.

She sipped, but she coughed so violently that the priest removed the glass. Will saw a gush of blood run from the young woman's mouth. He wished he had the linen cloth from church to wipe the blood away for her, but he didn't even have a handkerchief. Father Keegan wiped away the blood with a cloth that Mrs. Cameron handed to him.

"Will you promise me, Father?" the dying woman begged. "I will die in peace if I know my babe will be well looked after."

Father Keegan did not answer, and Will wondered why he hesitated.

"Do you wish me to hear your last confession, my daughter?"

With unexpected strength, the girl caught him by the sleeve. "Father, is it true that Our Lord is all-knowing? That He can see into every soul and forgive even the worst sins because He understands them? Is that the truth?"

"Yes, child, that is what Our Saviour Jesus Christ taught us. God sees everything."

She let go. "Thank you, Father, that is a comfort to me."

Those were the last words she would ever say.

Chapter Eleven

———

"Whew," said Wendy. "That is such a sad story. I think I'd like a cup of coffee, Dad."

"Okay. I'll make it. And I'll check on Amy."

Bill did so, and it looked like Amy was quite content to sit with Boots in front of her cartoons. He had been right to fear that his story was too grown up for her. She'd made a good choice.

Bill went back upstairs to Wendy. She sipped some of the coffee, then leaned back in bed. Bill remembered again how he had read stories to her when she was a little girl. Watching her with her rumpled hair and her nose already getting red from her cold, his heart melted.

She smiled at him. "Go on, Dad. I'm ready. We left off where the poor girl has died."

Father Keegan gave the young woman the Last Rites, the final ritual of prayer for a dying person. Then he got to his feet.

"Mrs. Cameron," he said to the midwife, "I will leave her to you. Come, Will. We have not yet finished."

William followed the priest back into the hall. He felt as if his heart was in a vice. Seeing the death of such a young and beautiful woman moved him deeply.

A soft hum of conversation rose from the end of the hall. Will saw his mother, and she smiled at him. He felt proud that she would see him performing such important tasks.

"We had better look for that money and make sure it's safe," said Father Keegan.

The two of them went over to one of the silent mounds. The priest removed the blanket that Saul had put over the body of the blond-haired man.

"Let's get the coat off him first."

Will had never touched a dead body before, and the feel of the cold, clammy skin almost turned his stomach. He was glad he'd had nothing to eat.

Underneath the coat, the man was wearing a thick woollen jersey and black serge trousers. Their damp sea-soaked smell filled Will's nostrils.

"This man is dressed like a sailor," Will said to the priest.

"Indeed he is." Father Keegan turned the man's hands palms-up and ran his finger over the rough skin. "He certainly has worked like one."

He felt along the hem of the coat, then quickly tore open the seam. Will held back his gasp of surprise. Gold coins flowed out onto the floor, more than he had ever seen in his life.

"No wonder he was such a heavy burden," said the priest. "And here we have something more." He removed a small purse of purple velvet. He untied the string that kept it closed and held the open purse out for Will to see. It was filled with diamonds. "This man did hard work. He could never earn this much wealth in ten lifetimes."

"Father, I don't understand. The lady said he saved her. You asked if the blond-haired man was her husband, and she said yes. She told us his name was John. But she is well-born. How could she marry a rough sailor like him?"

Father Keegan's expression was kind as he glanced at William.

"Such things do happen, my son, but in fact, she never answered my question. I noticed that at the time. I also thought her worry about whether we had spoken to anyone on board was strange."

Will stared at him, not entirely sure what this meant.

The priest continued. "I would bet that her real husband is lying right over there." He made his way over to the last body at the end of the row. He pulled away the tarp. The dead man was plump, with a neat beard, black as ink. It was an unnatural colour. He was dressed only in a shirt, vest, and trousers. Will noticed his boots. They were made of fine leather, with fashionable square toes.

"This man dyed his hair," said Father Keegan. "And he has the soft chin and round stomach of a well-fed man. He was no sailor. I would say he was the merchant who paid for his and his wife's trip." The priest leaned forward. "Look, Will, look at his shirt. What do you notice?"

They seemed to have slipped into the role of teacher and student, and Will liked it. Liked being able to please this sharp-tongued man.

Will moved in closer. "The cloth is of fine quality. It feels like pure linen. "

"Yes, but more important, see the tear in that fine shirt."

The priest unbuttoned the man's vest and opened the front of the shirt. He pointed to a small hole in the man's chest, visible even through the grey hair. "The sea has washed away the blood, but I would say that our merchant friend here was stabbed. The wound is a narrow one." The priest lifted the man's hands and ran his fingers across the palms. "Look at these cuts on both of his hands, and here, on the underside of his arm. What does that tell you, Will?"

Will lifted his own arms as if somebody was coming to attack him. "He got those cuts trying to defend himself."

"Quite right. Unfortunately for him, he wasn't successful."

"Do you think it was the sailor who killed him, Father? For his money?"

"Whoever killed him was not after his money. See, the merchant has a fine gold watch and chain in his vest. And yes, there are coins still in his pockets." The priest counted them. "Twenty dollars. This money was not touched, and the gold and diamonds were well hidden. But let us not excuse John, the sailor, just yet. Go and check his boots. See if he is carrying a knife. If he is, bring it to me."

Will, his heart racing, hurried to do as the priest asked. There was a leather sheath stuffed down the blond-haired man's right boot. Will removed it and returned to the priest. Father Keegan pulled out the knife, which was the kind fishermen used to prepare fish for market. The blade looked sharp and efficient.

"The sheath protected the blade in spite of the water. You can see that the blade is stained almost to the hilt. Even the sea could not wash away all the blood."

Father Keegan brought the tip of the blade close to the cut above the dead man's heart. The wound and the knife were the same width.

"I would say we have found our weapon."

William stared at him in dismay. "If the sailor is a murderer, surely the lady did not help him? She was so…"

He paused, and the priest smiled at him. "Young? Beautiful? History is filled with tales of women of great beauty who were black sinners. However, did you notice the old bruises turning yellow on her arm? And the severe bruise on the side of her face? That one was recent. But she did not get them when the ship ran into the rocks. Somebody had gripped her hard on the arm a while ago. Hard enough to bruise her. The other mark looks as if it was caused by a fist. As if someone hit her on the side of her face."

Will turned away. He didn't know if the priest knew what happened at home, but he suspected he did. His mother had been given such bruises more than once by her husband, his father, and Will was deeply ashamed of it.

"Look at this merchant," continued the priest. "He is many years older than the girl. What is he doing marrying such a child? He cannot have truly cared for her. A man who cherishes his wife would not bring her on a rough sea voyage when she is so close to having her baby. What business could be so important that she had to come with him? And on such an uncomfortable working vessel? This merchant had plenty of money. If he needed his wife to come with him, he could have afforded better."

Father Keegan paused. His voice was thoughtful. "Why did the merchant think he had to hide his gold and diamonds? Was he the kind of man who feels suspicious of everybody? Perhaps he saw his child wife the way he saw his diamonds and gold. An object to be guarded."

"Is it possible that she wanted to be on the voyage, Father?" asked Will. "It does seem as if her husband's killer was one of the crew. Perhaps she was the one who insisted on coming along. Perhaps she and the sailor thought they could easily get rid of the merchant while they were aboard a ship. Men fall overboard all the time."

Father Keegan chuckled. "William Murdoch, I am glad to hear you are not sentimental, even though you found the young woman so beautiful. What you have said is certainly possible. And her question to me, confirming that Our Lord understands everything and forgives everything. That was from her heart, was it not?"

Will nodded. "If she was guilty of murder, her words have a different meaning. On the other hand, the sailor may have scared her into helping him."

Again the priest smiled at his clever student. "If he had scared her, she would not have wept as she did when she heard he was dead." Father Keegan shook his head. "No, that does not fit what we have learned so far. She praised the sailor. She said that he saved her by giving up his place in the rowboat for her. That does not sound to me as if he frightened her."

Will frowned. "Perhaps the sailor gave up his place so he could go back below deck. Perhaps he wanted to steal the coat of the man he had just stabbed. The sailor didn't know that all of the crew would be drowned. It was safer for him to crawl onto the rocks and try to escape that way."

Father Keegan shook his head. "Perhaps he didn't even know there was gold hidden in the coat. He just wanted it to keep him warm. If that's true, he and the merchant's wife were not working together."

It was William's turn to grin. "I was only trying to look at every possibility, Father. As you say, not with the heart, but with the head."

"What else are you thinking?" asked the priest.

"We know this knife killed this man, but we do not know who used it. Even women can be sinners, as you said."

Father Keegan nodded. "But the reason and the heart must work together, Will. What does your heart say?"

William paused. "My heart tells me that what I have just said is nonsense. Worse than nonsense, if truth be told. Mistress Abigail was no murderer. For all we know, she may have hated the man who treated her so badly, but I don't think she would kill him."

"I think I agree with you, against all logic, of course," said the priest.

William was fast warming to his subject. He felt like an adult, all of a sudden, and he liked that feeling. "Mistress Abigail told us that she was alone in the world. She did not want anybody to claim her child. She may be an orphan, of course. But most people have someone they could pass their child to. So I believe that, in her married life, the young lady was alone. Perhaps those around her didn't like her. Perhaps they were jealous of her beauty and her wealthy husband."

Sometimes gossip in the village was about this very thing. A young pretty woman marrying an older man who had property and some wealth. She was the one who the villagers spoke about with disapproval, never the man.

"Very good, Will. Very good. That is not unlikely."

Will went on. "Mistress Abigail wanted her daughter to be raised by someone who would love her."

"Mary Ann Pierce will be a loving mother, I know it."

Will bit his lip. "Father, why did Mistress Abigail die?"

The priest raised his eyebrows. "Surely you do not want to discuss God's mysterious ways at this moment?"

"No, Father. But I am puzzled. Mistress Abigail bled from the mouth. The midwife said she thought the lady had some broken ribs. How did this happen? I have been tipped out of a boat more than once. I suffered no harm, except for a bellyful of salt water."

"Let's find out," said the priest. "Stay here."

Chapter Twelve

Father Keegan went over to the curtain and called to Mrs. Cameron, the midwife. Will couldn't hear what he was saying, but he saw how the woman acted. Mrs. Cameron was shocked at first, but then she agreed. The priest ducked under the curtain. Several minutes later, he emerged. He came over to Will, and his face was angry.

"You are a clever lad, William Murdoch. Her ribs were indeed broken. Her entire side was bruised. The marks of a boot were evident. A square-toed boot."

Will pointed. "That is what the merchant is wearing. John, the sailor, has on ordinary rubber sea boots."

Father Keegan stood looking down at the body of the rich man. "He hit her hard on the side of the face. Why we will never know, but clearly he had hit her before. When she fell to the floor, he began to kick her. Perhaps she screamed. The sailor came to her rescue. He took out the only weapon he had, his fishing knife. He stabbed the attacker. He may have hit the heart accidentally. If indeed a man as wicked as our merchant has a heart. The ship must have been sinking when this occurred. John Sailor helped Mistress Abigail to the deck and got her into the rowboat. He sacrificed his own life."

"Do you think the two of them knew each other before this?" Will asked.

The priest shrugged. "I don't know. Perhaps the sailor was simply a good man who would not stand by when he heard a woman cry for help. Whatever happened, their souls are in God's hands, and He will be their judge." He looked up. "Ah, there is Mary Ann Pierce now."

A young woman had come into the hall, a shawl over her head. Her body was still soft and full from being pregnant. Her face showed her grief for her dead baby. Mrs. Cameron came from behind the curtain, the newborn in her arms. She handed the baby to the other woman. Immediately, Mary Ann Pierce brought the little one close inside her shawl. Her sad face came alive with joy. She rocked the infant tenderly.

The priest sighed. "I had feared for Mary Ann's mind, her grief was so large. I do believe she will be all right now." He poked at the pile of gold coins. "Mistress Abigail, in her innocence, thought I could deal with this treasure by myself. And with her child. Alas, I cannot. The court will have to trace the merchant's family, and they will have a claim on the money and diamonds." He picked up a couple of the gold coins. "On Christmas Day, however, we should present our newborn child with a gift. This will be enough money to help Mrs. Pierce care for the baby until somebody comes for her. Who knows? The merchant's family may decide they do not want an orphan child, and Mrs. Pierce will be able to keep her."

Father Keegan watched Mary Ann Pierce for a few moments as she cooed to the baby in her arms. His expression was more sad than happy. William wondered what he was remembering.

Chapter Thirteen

Bill put down his story. At that moment, Amy came into the room. She jumped onto the bed and snuggled up to her mother.

"What happened to the baby, Dad?" asked Wendy.

"Will guessed right. The young mother was not well liked by her husband's family and had been treated badly. When her in-laws finally came to the village, they wanted nothing to do with her baby. They were only too happy to leave the little one with the village woman, Mary Ann Pierce. As long as they got most of the money. In the end, the child was dearly loved, and she grew up to be a beautiful and good woman."

"So when did great-great-great-grandfather become a policeman?" asked Amy.

"After he left school, he went west. He was a lumberjack for a while, cutting down trees. Then he came to Toronto and joined the police force. Eventually, he became a detective. He had a gift for police work. He had the ability to put the pieces of a puzzle together. Also, he was the kind of man who refused to give up. He always wanted justice, especially for those who had nobody else to look after them."

Amy grinned. "I'm going to be a detective when I grow up."

"Last night you said you wanted to be a midwife and help bring babies into the world," said Wendy.

"I'll do that first, before I become a detective. Is that everything, Granddad? Is that the end of the story?"

"Yes, that's it."

"Can we all play cards now? Do you want to, Mommy?"

"Sure."

"I'll join you in a minute," said Bill.

He went over to the window. It was grey and cold outside. The wind shook the trees. It was in weather like this that the ship had crashed on the rocks so many years ago.

Bill hadn't been looking forward to Christmas without his wife, but suddenly he felt differently. He had a daughter whom he loved. When did he last tell her that? Not for a while, he thought. He had been so caught up in his own sadness that he hadn't paid enough attention to Wendy. She had lost the mother she loved.

Bill began to think. Wendy's house was small; his house was much roomier. What if Wendy and Amy came to live with him? It would be easy to turn the basement into a nice apartment where he could live. Wendy and Amy could live in the rest of the house. He would even learn to forgive Keith, if Wendy decided to get back together with him.

He turned back to look at his daughter and granddaughter. He smiled. Everybody needs a warm, safe place that is full of love. It is called a home.

Good ■ Reads

Discover Canada's Bestselling Authors with Good Reads Books

Good Reads authors have a special talent—
the ability to tell a great story, using clear language.

Good Reads books are ideal for people

✳ on the go, who want a short read;
✳ who want to experience the joy of reading;
✳ who want to get into the reading habit.

To find out more, please visit
www.GoodReadsBooks.com

The Good Reads project is sponsored by
ABC Life Literacy Canada.

The project is funded in part by the Government of Canada's
Office of Literacy and Essential Skills.

Libraries and literacy and education markets
order from Grass Roots Press.

Bookstores and other retail outlets order from HarperCollins Canada.

Good Reads Series

If you enjoyed this Good Reads book,
you can find more at your local library or bookstore.

2010

The Stalker by Gail Anderson-Dargatz
In From the Cold by Deborah Ellis
Shipwreck by Maureen Jennings
The Picture of Nobody by Rabindranath Maharaj
The Hangman by Louise Penny
Easy Money by Gail Vaz-Oxlade

2011 Authors

Joseph Boyden
Marina Endicott
Joy Fielding
Robert Hough
Anthony Hyde
Frances Itani

*

For more information on Good Reads,
visit **www.GoodReadsBooks.com**

The Hangman
by Louise Penny

On a cold November morning, a jogger runs through the woods in the peaceful Quebec village of Three Pines. On his run, he finds a dead man hanging from a tree.

The dead man was a guest at the local Inn and Spa. He might have been looking for peace and quiet, but something else found him. Something horrible.

Did the man take his own life? Or was he murdered? Chief Inspector Armand Gamache is called to the crime scene. As Gamache follows the trail of clues, he opens a door into the past. And he learns the true reason why the man came to Three Pines.

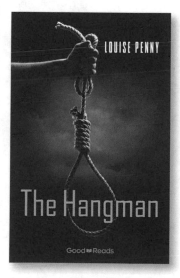

The Stalker
by Gail Anderson-Dargatz

Very early one Saturday morning, Mike's phone rings. "Nice day for a little kayak trip, eh?" says the deep, echoing voice. "But I wouldn't go out if I were you."

Mike's business is guiding visitors on kayak tours around the islands off the west coast. This weekend, he'll be taking Liz, his new cook, and two strangers on a kayak tour. Soon, his phone rings again. "I'm watching you," the caller says. "Stay home."

Mike and the others set off on their trip, but the

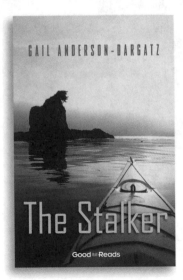

stalker secretly follows them. Who is he? What will he do? *The Stalker* will keep you guessing until the end.

In From the Cold
by Deborah Ellis

Rose and her daughter Hazel are on the run in a big city. During the day, Rose and Hazel live in a shack hidden in the bushes. At night, they look for food in garbage bins.

In the summer, living in the shack was like an adventure for Hazel. But now, winter is coming and the nights are cold.

Hazel is starting to miss her friends and her school. Rose is trying to do the right thing for her daughter, but everything is going so wrong. Will Hazel stay loyal to her mother, or will she try to return to her old life?

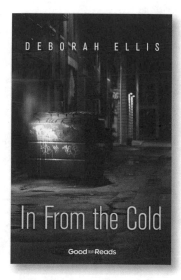

Easy Money
by Gail Vaz-Oxlade

Wish you could find a money book that doesn't make your eyes glaze over or your brain hurt? Easy Money is for you.

Gail knows you work hard for your money, so in her usual honest and practical style she will show you how to make your money work for you. Budgeting, saving, and getting your debt paid off have never been so easy to understand or to do. Follow Gail's plan and take control of your money.

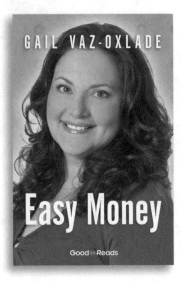

The Picture of Nobody
by Rabindranath Maharaj

Tommy lives with his family in Ajax, a small town close to Toronto. His parents are Ismaili Muslims who immigrated to Canada before Tommy was born. Tommy, a shy, chubby seventeen-year-old, feels like an outsider.

The arrest of a terrorist group in Toronto turns Tommy's world upside down. No one noticed him before. Now, he experiences the sting of racism at the local coffee shop where he works part-time. A group of young men who hang out at the coffee shop begin to bully him. In spite, Tommy commits an act of revenge against the group's ringleader.

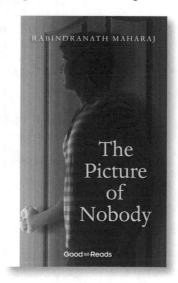

About the Author

 Maureen Jennings is the author of the Detective Murdoch mysteries. These mysteries are set in Toronto, during the 1890s. The award-winning *Murdoch Mysteries* TV series is based on Maureen's novels. Maureen was born in England and immigrated to Canada in 1956. She lives in Toronto with her husband, two dogs, and two cats.

Also by Maureen Jennings:

The Detective Murdoch Mysteries

Except the Dying
Under the Dragon's Tail
Poor Tom Is Cold
Let Loose the Dogs
Night's Child
Vices of My Blood
A Journeyman to Grief

You can visit Maureen's website at
www.maureenjennings.com